TICKLE ME
My Name Is ELMO

by **Constance Allen** • illustrated by **Maggie Swanson**

Featuring Jim Henson's Sesame Street Muppets
Originally published as My Name Is Elmo

 A GOLDEN BOOK • NEW YORK
Golden Books Publishing Company, Inc., Racine, Wisconsin 53404

Published by Golden Books Publishing Company, Inc., in cooperation with Children's Television Workshop

A portion of the money you pay for this book goes to Children's Television Workshop.
It is put right back into SESAME STREET and other CTW educational projects. Thanks for helping!

Hello! Elmo is so happy to see you! Welcome to Sesame Street!

This is Elmo's room. See outside? There's Oscar's trash can. Hi, Oscar! And over there is Big Bird's nest. Hello, Big Bird!

See this hat? It's a firefighter's hat! Maybe when Elmo grows up, Elmo will be a firefighter. Yeah.

This is Elmo's bed. This is Elmo's favorite
teddy monster. And this is Elmo's favorite poster.

Do you want to make funny faces? Come on!
Let's make funny faces!

Did you know that furry little red monsters are very ticklish? Tickle Elmo's toes!
    Ha! Ha! Ha! That tickles!

Do you want to know Elmo's favorite color?
It's yellow! And blue! And red and pink and green
and orange and purple! Elmo likes all colors. Yay!

This is Elmo's friend Ernie. Sometimes we play horsie. Wheeeee! Giddyap, Ernie!

Elmo drew a picture. Do you want to see it?
Okay! Turn the page, and you can see Elmo's
picture!

Here it is! See? Maybe
Elmo will be a firefighter
and an artist when he
grows up.

Elmo will now show you a trick. Are you ready?
Watch. Are you watching? Okay, Elmo will now
bend over like this . . .

and everything will be upside down!
See? Now you try it.

This is Big Bird. We're friends. Sometimes we try to chase each other's shadows like this.

Peekaboo!
Ha! Ha!

Here is one of Elmo's
favorite games:

Here's Elmo's favorite number: 4. There are four letters in Elmo's name, and four wheels on Elmo's bike. Elmo has four toy cars. And Elmo's pet turtle, Walter, has four feet.

Elmo likes to meet new people. When he meets them, this is what Elmo says. . . .

Hello! Elmo is so happy to meet you!